Frogs

by Bobby Lynn Maslen
pictures by John R. Maslen

Scholastic Inc.
New York • Toronto • London • Auckland • Sydney • Mexico City • New Delhi • Hong Kong • Buenos Aires

Available Bob Books®:

Set 1: Beginning Readers — With consistent new sounds added gradually, your new reader is gently introduced to all the letters of the alphabet. They can soon say, "I read the whole book!®"

Set 2: Advancing Beginners — The use of three-letter words and consistent vowel sounds in slightly longer stories build skill and confidence.

Set 3: Word Families — Consonant blends, endings and a few sight words advance reading skills while the use of word families keep reading manageable.

Set 4: Compound Words — Longer books and complex words engage young readers as proficiency advances.

Set 5: Long Vowels — Silent *e* and other vowel blends build young readers' vocabulary and aptitude.

Bob Books® Collections:

Collection 1 — Includes Set 1: Beginning Readers and part of Set 2: Advancing Beginners

Collection 2 — Includes part of Set 2: Advancing Beginners and Set 3: Word Families

Collection 3 — Includes Set 4: Compound Words and Set 5: Long Vowels

Ask for Bob Books at your local bookstore, or visit www.bobbooks.com.

ISBN 0-545-02690-3

6 5 4 3 2 1 7 8 9 10 11/0

Printed in China
This edition first printing, September 2007

Mama Frog and Papa Frog
sat on a log.

Ten polliwogs swam in the pond.

A bird was in the pond.

The bird
was big
and tall.

The bird saw the polliwogs and frogs.

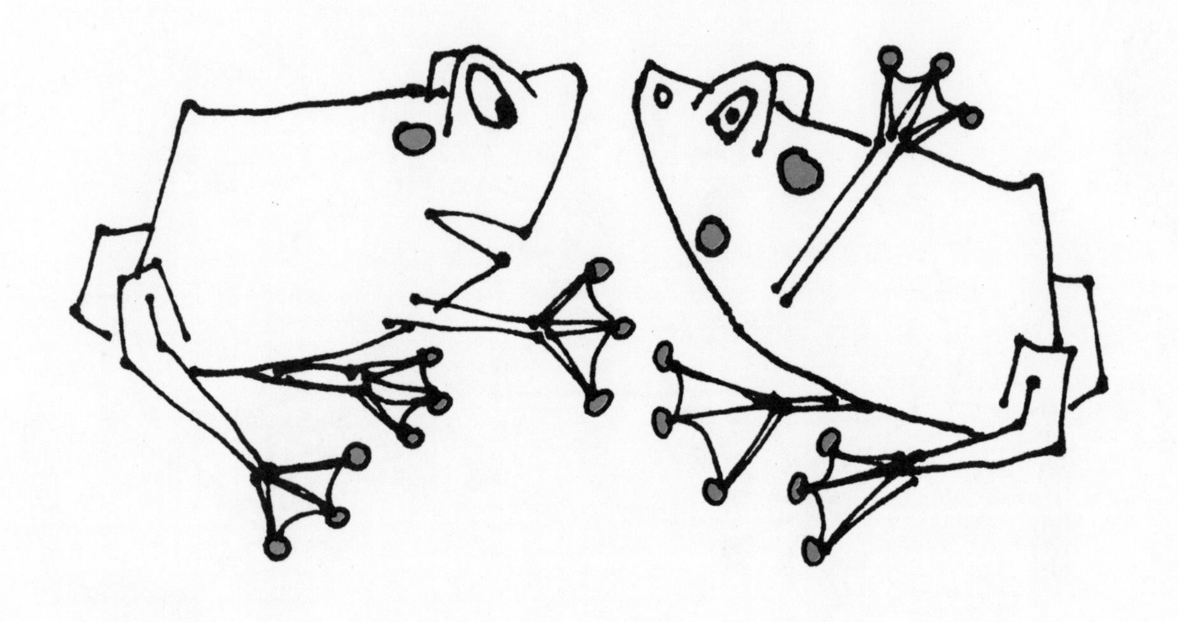

"Birds eat polliwogs,

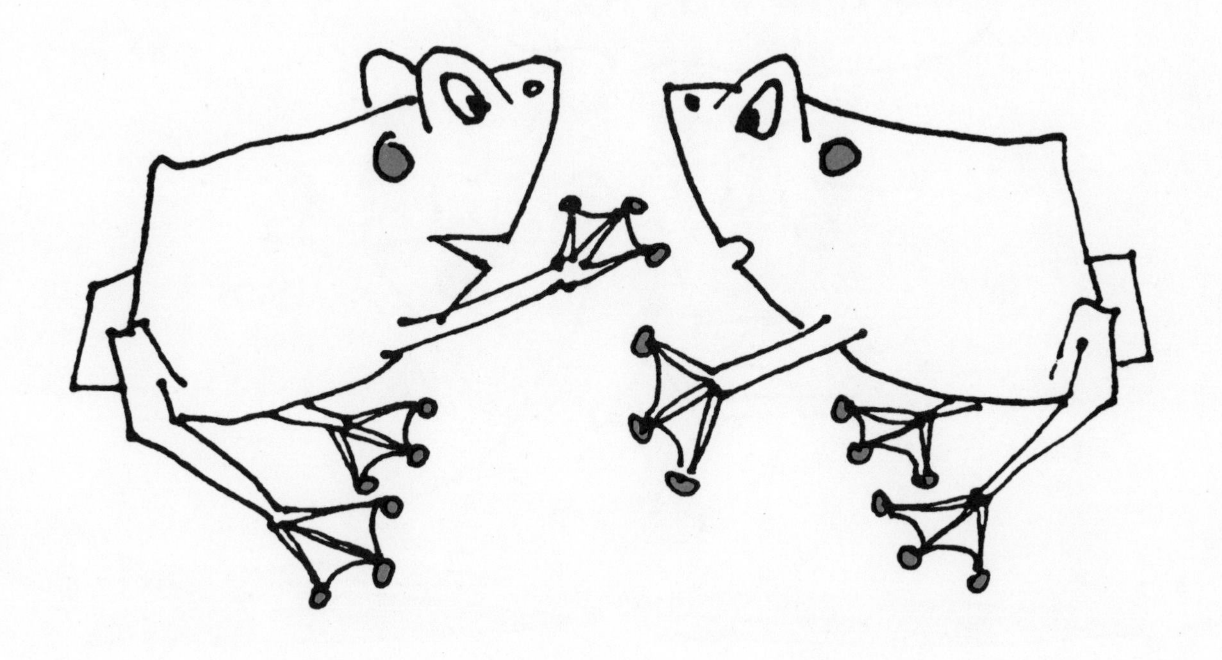

birds eat frogs," said Papa Frog.

"Jump! Hide!" said Papa.

"Swim! Dive!" said Mama.

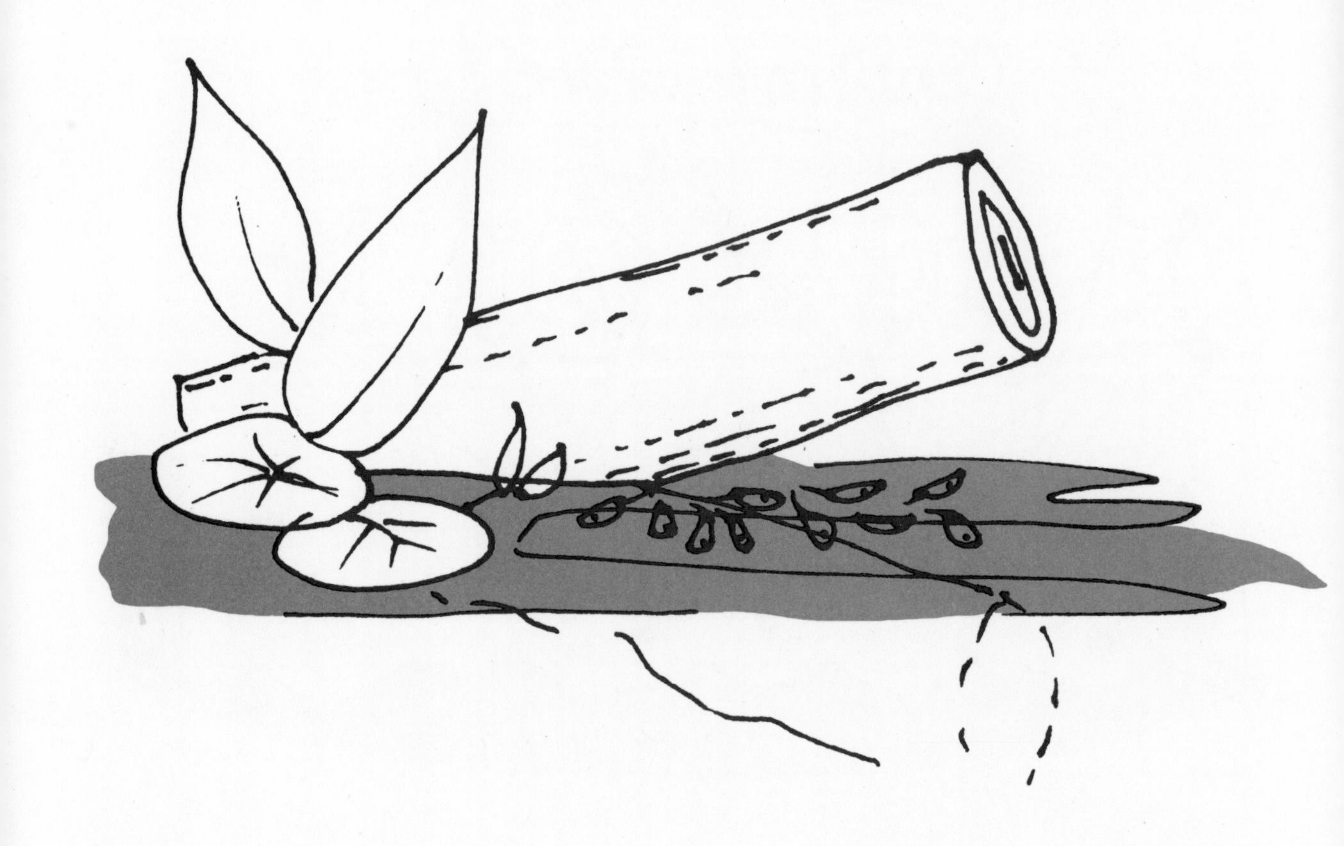

The wogs went under a log.

The frogs went under a log.

So for dinner the bird had a big hot dog.

The End

List of 35 words in Frogs

Short Vowels

a	e	i	o	u	sight
and	ten	in	on	jump	a
had	went	big	hot	under	so
sat	end	swim	dog		saw
swam		dinner	log		was
			frog		the
			pond		tall
			polliwogs		bird
			wogs		said
					Mama
					Papa
					for

Long Vowels

eat
dive
hide

75 total words in *Frogs*